For Clancy and his many pandas, with thanks to Mr P. D. Eastman — **KATE & JOL**

For Niharika and Shay — **RONOJOY**

Published by Allen & Unwin in 2018

Text copyright © Kate and Jol Temple 2018
Illustrations copyright © Ronojoy Ghosh 2018

Allen & Unwin
83 Alexander Street
Crows Nest NSW 2065
Australia
Phone: (61 2) 8425 0100
Email: info@allenandunwin.com
Web: www.allenandunwin.com

 A catalogue record for this
book is available from the
National Library of Australia

ISBN 978 1 76063 164 2

For teaching resources, explore www.allenandunwin.com/
resources/for-teachers

Text and cover design by Liz Seymour
Set in 19 pt Mandolin and Konga Pro

This book was printed in March 2018 by Hang Tai Printing
Company Limited, China

10 9 8 7 6 5 4 3 2 1

www.katejoltemple.com
www.ronojoyghosh.com.au

ARE YOU MY BOTTOM?

WRITTEN BY

Kate & Jol Temple

ILLUSTRATED BY

Ronojoy Ghosh

ALLEN & UNWIN
SYDNEY · MELBOURNE · AUCKLAND · LONDON

Something is missing, and I'm not sure what...
Oh dear, now I know it—I've lost my **BOT!**
When I went to sleep, it was definitely here
But today I woke up and I have **NO REAR!**

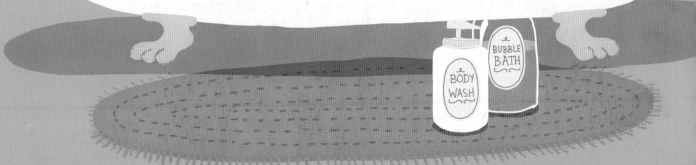

I've looked under a rock and under a chair.

It's not over **HERE** and it's not over **THERE**.

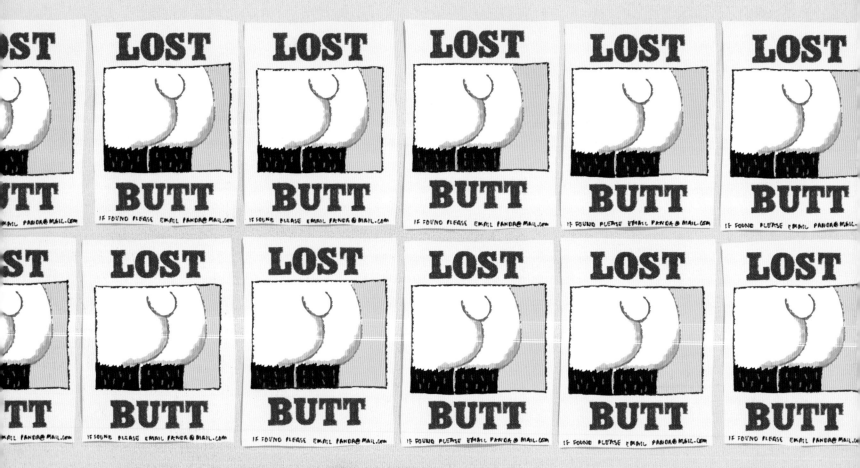

I've looked up high and I've looked down low

Where it has gone, I just do not know.

I've **FOUND** it! I've **FOUND** it!

I see it right there!

That's the runaway bot

of a small panda bear!

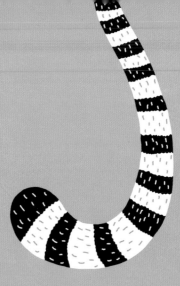

'No, little one, I'm not being unkind
But I am a **LEMUR**—this is my behind.'
I see that now. What a terrible fail!
You have such a beautiful, long, stripy tail.
I'll just keep looking. I'll find it, you'll see...

AH HA! Is that it? Up that prickle-thorn tree?
It looks like it could be, but something's not right...
Why is my bottom at such a **GREAT HEIGHT?**

'Oh dear, small panda, don't be absurd.

This is the bum of a fine-feathered **BIRD**.'

Alright there, old tweeter, now don't get so cranky.

It's true your behind is rather too swanky.

My bottom will be here. It can't have gone far

And I must say this whole thing is rather bizarre.

And look—I've seen it!

Under that pine!

It's soft. It's furry. **THAT BOTTOM IS MINE!**

'No, no, small friend. This is not your caboose.
This is the bum of a long-legged **MOOSE**.'
Oh dear. It is true. Your bottom's too grey.
I must keep looking—I'll go now, good day!

I've searched many places, even up a big tree.
But still I can't find it! Oh, where could it be?
AH HA! I've found it, there's my cheeky botty!
Only, I wonder—should it be so spotty?

'Oh, stop it, young panda, you're making me laugh!
  This bot here is mine, and I'm a **GIRAFFE!**'

Quite right, I see you've got all of those blotches!
  It can't be my bottom, for I've never had splotches.

I want my bot back and I'm starting to worry.
  Where has it gone? I must find it—and hurry!

Mystery solved! There it is!

THERE'S MY BUM!

It's looking quite pink...

has it been in the sun?

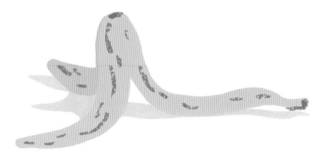

'Little bear, I'm afraid
you have spoken too soon.
This is MY fancy bottom
and I'm a **BABOON**.'

I give up. It's gone. My bot's simply not here.

So now I'm the panda without any rear.

Nothing to soften a stumble or fall

Nothing to sit on, or scritch-scratch at all.

BUT WAIT! What's that with all the black hair?

Could it be the bot of a small panda bear?

It's furry, it's black, with even some white.

This bottom's the one! It's **DEFINITELY** right!

'Oh, little panda,

now you've gone too far!

This bottom's too **HUGE**—

it belongs to your Pa!

It never would fit,

you'd end up in a flummox

Yours is right where

you left it...

YOUR SMALL PANDA BUMMOX.

KATE and **JOL** are award-winning children's authors. Their picture books include I Got This Hat, Mike I Don't Like and Room On Our Rock. Their chapter book series Captain Jimmy Cook Discovers Third Grade was selected as Honour Book by the Children's Book Council of Australia. They live in Sydney with their two sons and several small pandas. This is their first book about bottoms, probably their last.

RONOJOY GHOSH has worked in India, Indonesia, Singapore and New Zealand, and currently lives in Australia with his wife and son. Beyond his award-winning work in advertising, his passion lies in children's picture books. He is the writer and illustrator of Ollie and the Wind, shortlisted for the 2016 CBCA Book of the Year, and the illustrator of the 2018 CBCA notable book, I'm Australian, Too, written by Mem Fox.